Tick Tock Terror

Melanie Jackson

orca currents

ORCA BOOK PUBLISHERS

Library and Archives Canada Cataloguing in Publication

Jackson, Melanie, 1956–, author
Tick tock terror / Melanie Jackson.
(Orca currents)

Issued in print and electronic formats.
ISBN 978-1-4598-1955-9 (softcover).—ISBN 978-1-4598-1956-6 (PDF).—
ISBN 978-1-4598-1957-3 (EPUB)

I. Title. II. Series: Orca currents
PS8569.A265T53 2019 jC813'.6 C2018-904894-8
C2018-904895-6

First published in the United States, 2019
Library of Congress Control Number: 2018954095

Summary: In this high-interest novel for middle readers, Conor gets in over his head when he agrees to hide a mysterious package at the top of an amusement park ride.

MIX
Paper from responsible sources
FSC® C016245

Orca Book Publishers is dedicated to preserving the environment and has printed this book on Forest Stewardship Council® certified paper.

Orca Book Publishers gratefully acknowledges the support for its publishing programs provided by the following agencies: the Government of Canada, the Canada Council for the Arts and the Province of British Columbia through the BC Arts Council and the Book Publishing Tax Credit.

Edited by Tanya Trafford
Cover photography by iStock.com/Fyletto
Author photo by Bart Jackson

ORCA BOOK PUBLISHERS
orcabook.com

Printed and bound in Canada.

22 21 20 19 • 4 3 2 1

Let my heart be still a moment and
this mystery explore...

—Edgar Allan Poe, "The Raven"

Chapter One

Tick...

The giant, curved blade sliced high into the air. Swung by a steel chain, the blade soared to 140 feet.

In the seats at the top of the blade, passengers screamed. They were terrified the ride was going to hurl them into outer space.

The blade sliced back down, then zoomed its riders up the other side.

Tock...

All day every day at the amusement park the Pendulum's loudspeakers blasted out that ominous *tick...*then *tock...*

Like a countdown to doom.

Or at least to losing your lunch.

I knew the feeling. I'd been on the Pendulum, the newest thrill ride at Vancouver's Playland. I'd been on all the rides. Cliff Edge, the climbing gym where I worked, was across the street. I came over on my lunch hours.

The Pendulum plunged again. It whipped across the sandpit at its base. The sharp, shiny blade missed the body lying face up, chained to the ground, by inches.

The ride was based on the Edgar Allan Poe story "The Pit and the Pendulum."

In the story, set in 1400s Spain, a man gets on the wrong side of the law. As punishment his torturers swing a blade-edged pendulum over him.

The torturers slowly lower the weight closer. At first the crescent-shaped blade just tickles his chest. Then scrapes it. Then—

Let's just call it the slice-and-dice approach to revenge.

The body in the sandpit is a dummy. But its face, twisted in agony, is very realistic. So are the bloodstains on its chest.

What kind of person would you have to be to dream up a story like that? Edgar Allan must have been one miserable guy.

I stopped thinking about Poe and the Pendulum. I gazed up at the horizontal bar the chain was swinging from.

Two vertical bars supported the horizontal one on either side. At the top the vertical bars curved together. Towering over the park, the structure looked like a big black upside-down U.

Or like a doorway to the bright blue sky beyond…

I heard a hoarse, wavering voice. "Think you could climb it?"

I jumped. Who had said that? Had they guessed what I was thinking. About how great it would be to climb the upside-down U up to that horizontal bar. To leave everything behind so it was just me and endless sky.

Because it wasn't enough for me to look up at a building or statue or tree. I had to get to the top. Or at least imagine getting to the top.

I looked around. I couldn't see anyone paying attention to me. People were chatting, laughing. Thinking about their next ride or giant cone of candy floss.

From the tunnel-shaped walkway leading to the Pendulum, a laugh cackled out. A bent old man winked at me from a side door.

I remembered him. He was the ride attendant who helped people in and out of their seats. I thought he was a bit frail to have a job like that.

The old man shuffled up to me. I noticed he was wearing faded red slippers. His badge, curved like the Pendulum blade, read *Victor Varken, Manager*.

He stank of cigarette smoke. I remembered that too.

"I was at Cliff Edge this morning," he said. "I saw how you climbed. You were lighter than the air."

I had never heard it put like that. I liked it. *Lighter than the air*.

Aside from the occasional growl of approval, my boss at Cliff Edge never complimented me that way. He knew I was an ace climber. That's why he hired me for the summer.

But he worried about me. He thought I was too confident about my climbing. *Stupid*-confident, he called me.

I pushed my boss out of my mind.

I started to thank the old man for his compliment. But before I could, he broke into a coughing fit that shook his frail frame. Even his wispy white hair bounced.

What had such an unhealthy, out-of-shape guy been doing at a gym? I couldn't imagine him scrambling up the wall holds. To climb you had to breathe slowly, steadily, deeply. You had to be fit.

Varken finally stopped coughing. He spat into the grass.

"Sir, you were a customer at Cliff Edge?" I asked.

"No, sonny. I went out for a smoke this morning. They won't let me smoke in the park. Eyes on me everywhere, staring, judging!" The old man's face was red with rage. With an effort he calmed down. "I passed by Cliff Edge, saw you through the window."

He lowered his voice and continued. "The way you flew up the wall—you're the lad I need. I want to hire you for a one-time, secret climbing job. You'll go up the Pendulum tonight. When you get to the top, you'll hide a package for me."

Victor Varken stood on red-slippered tiptoes. He hissed, "Three hundred dollars, cash. No questions asked. I don't even want to know your name. You do it, you forget about it. Interested?"

If I was smart I would have walked away right then. But I wasn't smart. I was full of myself.

At Cliff Edge, when groups of kids visited, I hammed it up. Scaling the wall, I shouted down to them that I was the Climbing Fiend. *Nobody but nobody outclimbs the Fiend!*

The kids laughed. They loved it. But my boss was right about me. I *was* too confident. I actually did believe I was the Climbing Fiend, unbeatable, invincible.

So, trapped by my Mount Everest-sized ego, I stood there and listened to Varken.

Besides, I could use the extra money. Some buddies and I hoped to get away for a week in August. We wanted to go camping in Howe Sound, north of Vancouver. We planned to climb the Malamute, the white granite cliff by the water.

Wall holds at Cliff Edge and other gyms are fine for practice. But there is nothing like climbing real rock. The sun on you instead of artificial lights. The forever sky instead of a plaster ceiling.

The Pendulum's *tick...tock...* snapped me out of my Malamute daydream. I did a mental free fall into reality. Scaling the Pendulum would be trespassing. It could get me arrested.

"Forget it," I said.

Varken sank his bony fingers into my arm. "You *afraid* to climb?"

Chapter Two

Oh, smart guy. Play to my ego.

"I'm not afraid to climb anything," I said.

The old man cackled. He had just won, and he knew it. "Attaboy. And like I said just now? No questions. I don't even want to know your name. Once you do the climb, we forget our little deal ever happened."

I wrenched my arm away. "Listen, mister. I'm actually not sure I want to—"

"I have a package for you to hide up there." Varken pointed to the horizontal bar, which was about a hundred feet high, five feet wide. It would be a good hiding place. No one would see the package from the ground.

Varken stuck a match between his teeth, chewed on it. "Meet me by the gate at two AM."

"I'll be asleep," I snapped.

I stopped myself from adding, *And probably having nightmares about you.*

Varken fished in a back pocket. He brought out a stack of folded twenties. He pressed them into my hand.

I gaped at the bills. He had doubled the amount. Six hundred dollars would easily cover a trip to the Malamute. Some new climbing gear too.

But I held out the bills. "I can't take these. I can't do it."

"You *can't*?" Varken said with a sneer.

"I won't."

His gray face twisted into a nasty grin. "Yeah, you will. Or else I tell the cops that you stole that money from me."

I laughed. It was too absurd to take seriously.

I grabbed for Varken's wrist, trying to stuff the bills into his hand.

But he ducked. He speed-shuffled back to the walkway door.

The effort of moving so fast set him coughing again. Unable to speak, he held up two fingers.

Yeah, I got the message. Two AM.

"Not going to happen!" I called.

I had to return his money. I ran to the door.

Too late. Varken slammed it shut, though not before spitting a long stream into the grass.

I tried the handle. Locked.

I rubbed my arm where the old man's fingers had dug in. What was in the package he wanted me to stash up there? Hadn't the crazy old dude ever heard of safety deposit boxes?

The situation didn't seem so funny now. Maybe he'd meant it about going to the police if I didn't make the climb. About telling them I had stolen the money.

In the bright sun, all of a sudden I felt cold.

I shook it off. My lunch hour was up. I needed to get back to Cliff Edge.

I would come back after six, shove Varken's money at him. I could handle him, easy.

After all, he was just an old man.

Back at work, the boss was trying to lead a bunch of visiting day campers in song.

"*B-I-N-G-O, and Bingo was his name-oh*," Mr. Hogg sang. At the "*O*," the six-year-old campers winced and covered their ears. Hogg was hopelessly off-key.

Hogg—spelled with an extra *g* but pronounced plain old "hog"—spotted me.

"Take over," he muttered, wiping sweat off his forehead with a spare Cliff Edge T-shirt. "Kids! Ugh. They'll be the death of me."

I laughed. It was hard to imagine anything being the death of Hogg. He was an older guy, but lean, wiry and buff from climbing. He glowed with health like a shiny apple.

Hogg bought a power drink from the pop machine. He headed to his office to chug back the drink and chill.

I could see that a small ginger-haired kid was sitting in Hogg's office chair. Not just sitting. Spinning around so fast he was a blur.

I couldn't blame the kid. That had to be more fun than listening to my boss mangle the "Bingo" song.

Hogg seized the back of the chair. "Merry-go-round is over," he growled.

Ginger Hair's eyes widened in fright. He raced back to the group and plopped down in front of me.

It was time for my act.

I put on the blue cape my mom had made for me. She'd sewn the words *Climbing Fiend*, in glittery letters, on the back.

Hogg rolled back in his chair and put his feet on the desk. He watched me with what I guess was a mix of pride and exasperation.

He liked that I entertained our junior visitors with an act as opposed to just a straight demo. But he didn't like the Climbing Fiend part. *What, you're a comic-book hero?* He didn't think climbing was something to joke about. Joking led to accidents.

I bowed to the kids. I thumped my chest. "Nobody but nobody outclimbs the Fiend."

The kids were mesmerized. Did I mean it? Was I really the Fiend?

I started to climb. That stuff with Varken had given me surplus energy. To work it off I took the toughest way up.

I climbed the red holds, the ones that veered up the fifty-foot wall in a crazy diagonal. They were also spaced widely apart, harder to reach. Only the most seasoned climbers took this route.

But I could do it. I could climb anything.

Glancing down, I saw Hogg's uneasy expression. He didn't like that I'd gone for the red holds.

I realized what else he wasn't liking. I was climbing high without safety gear. I should have been wearing a harness. A rope from that harness would loop over a metal bar close to the ceiling. For this kind of climb, Hogg would be on the floor, holding the other end of the rope.

Normally I didn't wear safety gear for my act. It was clunky-looking. It detracted from my caped-climber routine. Hogg was okay with that—as long as I only climbed eight feet. That was our agreement.

If I fell eight feet, I'd bounce on the foamy floor. I'd be fine. From higher than eight feet, a fall became more *smash* than *bounce*.

Today, with angry energy inside,

I had forgotten our deal. I was more like fifteen feet up.

I stopped. But I was too much of a ham to resist goofing around. With my right hand I let go of a hold. I clasped my forehead like I was confused.

"What color am I on?" I called down to the kids. "Green? Orange? I forget! Help the Fiend out with this!"

They shrieked with laughter. "Red, Fiend! You're on *red*!"

Hogg shouted, "You know what you are, Conor Marlowe? An idiot!"

The kids laughed harder. They thought Hogg was kidding.

I knew he wasn't. I decided to give his nerves a break. I climbed down.

On the floor again I got serious with the kids. I told them, "Never climb on your own. Always have someone with you, watching out for you. It's important for climbers to follow *all* the safety rules. Remember that, okay?"

The kids nodded.

My boss looked skeptical. I saw it in his eyes—he didn't trust *me* to remember the rules.

He didn't trust me to keep myself safe.

Chapter Three

The kids got a turn to climb. They happily ran toward the five-foot-high kids' wall.

Most of them had no fear. They scrambled up their wall like mountain goats. If they fell, they did it on purpose so they could bounce.

Ginger Hair held back. He chewed on his lower lip.

I knelt beside him. "Be careful. You might chew that lip off."

He scowled. He stuck out his lower lip to show that it was still in one piece. Then he started chomping on it again.

I said, "Some people are afraid to climb. They come here, look at the walls and then go home again."

The kid shrugged. His gaze was fixed on his little buddies.

I said casually, "When I was a kid I was afraid *not* to climb."

He looked at me. He still didn't speak. But I was pretty sure he was interested.

I told him how I'd gotten into climbing. Not the usual ways. Not through lessons or seeing documentaries about Sir Edmund Hillary, the first person to reach the top of Mount Everest. All that came after.

I had been the new kid in our neighborhood. On the way home from school I passed an older boy kicking a garbage can around. He was huge. Later on I found out he had a nickname that fit him perfectly. Bull.

I watched Bull go to kick the can again. Instead he tripped over it.

"Good one, twinkle-toes!" I called.

Not the greatest idea to make fun of a human bull. But I couldn't help it. I snapped out wisecracks like some people pop bubblegum.

Bull started to chase me.

I tried running. His feet just pounded closer. I knew I couldn't escape. I stopped, looked around for help. There was no one else on the street.

Watching him racing toward me was too scary. I had to look away.

I looked up.

A giant chestnut tree towered over me, its thick, leafy branches spreading for yards.

Without even thinking, I shot up the trunk. Not smoothly, not the way I climb now. That day I clawed, clutched and shinned my way up. When I reached the first branch my hands, arms and legs were bleeding from bark scrapes.

But I escaped Bull. He glared up at me. He tried to start climbing after me. I wasn't worried. I could just scramble up to higher, lighter branches that would have broken under his weight.

Bull left.

After that he still chased me sometimes. No big deal. I kept practicing my climbing. I got better at it. I sat on a branch, swung my legs and yelled wisecracks down at him.

He couldn't catch me. No one could. I had my personal escape route from the world.

Up.

After listening to my story, Ginger Hair gave climbing a try. Turned out he liked it.

"No Bull!" he yelled as he and the other kids left.

The counselors winced. "Such language," one of them scolded.

The kids hopped into their day-camp van. I got a broom and swept up the crumbs from their snacks.

I glanced out the window. Across the street I could see the Pendulum hurling a fresh load of passengers high into the air. Even from here I could hear the ominous *tick...tock...*

It wasn't six o'clock yet. I wondered what time Varken quit for the day. I was determined to shove his money back at him.

Hogg noticed me looking out the window. "You don't want to be here, Marlowe? You got a big date?"

"No, sir." I kept sweeping. Much as I wanted to leave early, there was no point in asking. Hogg insisted on a thorough cleanup at the end of the day.

Which made his next remark surprising.

"You need to go do something, Marlowe? Go on. Get out of here."

I hesitated. There were still the washrooms to clean. But he waved his arms. "I told you to take off. Go!"

I parked the broom against a wall. What a decent guy, to break his own rule and let me off early.

I trudged out. Hogg was always warning me about my arrogance, my stupid confidence. If I had listened once, just once, I wouldn't have let Varken play me. I wouldn't be in this stupid mess.

The mess I now had to fix.

In my back pocket I could feel Varken's bills weighing down my wallet.

Stupid, stupid, stupid.

It was ten to six. The last people in the Pendulum lineup pushed through the turnstile. A girl in jeans and a Pendulum T-shirt was dragging the steel-barred doorway shut behind them.

"Wait!" I yelled.

The girl stopped. Her dark eyes widened with recognition.

Prisha Collins.

Just when I thought the day couldn't get worse.

Pree, as everyone called her, was my next-door neighbor. Her family had moved in the previous year. Mrs. Collins asked me to walk her daughter to and from school for the first while. Like she was a shy butterfly or something. Shy! Pree may have looked sweet and innocent. But she had all the shyness of a guided missile. And she could be a real pest.

Now, at the turnstile, Pree demanded, in her typical mile-a-minute style, "What's the big rush, Conor? What's going on?"

I rolled my eyes skyward. No Prishas up there. Another good reason to climb.

I silently counted to five. I made my voice reasonable. Not friendly. Friendly I couldn't manage.

"I don't have time to chat with you, Pree. I need to find Victor Varken."

"I can help you with that."

I stared. Pree helpful as opposed to annoying? That took a moment to get used to.

Pree nodded. "There was a posting for two students to help with the Pendulum. One of the jobs was to set up displays. I applied. I got the job a few days ago."

I could see why the park would hire Pree. A pest-onality like hers would be super efficient. That high-beam gaze wouldn't miss a thing. That yappity voice would nag out reminders nonstop.

I squinted down the dark tunnel. I could see some of the new displays, including a giant mechanical rat. Every few seconds the rat lurched forward and snapped its sharp white teeth.

We had studied "The Pit and the Pendulum" in school. In the story, normal-sized rats help the victim. They chew his ropes loose.

Pree walked ahead, her long dark ponytail doing its own pendulum-like swing. She tossed remarks back over her shoulder.

"My little brother loves your Fiend routine, by the way. His day camp visited Cliff Edge last week. At home he races up the stairs yelling, 'Nobody but nobody outclimbs the Fiend!'"

We passed the giant rat. I dodged its chomping teeth. "My boss isn't a Fiend fan. He thinks I should tone it down."

Pree turned to me. Now she wasn't laughing. "I'd trade your boss for mine any day. Victor doesn't want me around. He feels insulted that students were hired to help him. He says he doesn't need help. I think he's just mad because he can't smoke with us here."

I remembered Varken complaining about not being able to smoke. *Eyes on me everywhere, staring, judging!* And Pree had such an intense way of looking at people.

"He should thank you for making him cut back," I said.

She shook her head. "He just complains that I get in his way. And I've tried so hard, Conor. I spend hours looking up stuff about Poe. I make long lists of suggestions for the displays. And he uses them too. But it doesn't do any good. He still hates me."

She managed a smile. "Sorry to unload on you. I love the job. I want to work on set designs one day, either in theater or movies. So this job should be perfect. But... "

Her voice petered out. Normally I would have found the break in yakkity-yaks a relief. But this abrupt silence was so unlike Pree that it felt wrong. Like the natural order of things had been disturbed.

I hadn't thought it possible to dislike Varken more than I already did. But hearing how he mistreated Pree moved him from my dislike column into my hate one. What was his problem? She was conscientious. She was efficient. She cared about everything she did.

Just because I found her annoying didn't mean she deserved to be treated unfairly.

"Sounds like the Pendulum is the pits," I cracked weakly.

This made Pree smile a little bit. "I'll be okay, Conor. Like I said, I enjoy the work."

I was about to deliver another Varken insult. Then someone else did it for me.

"And his eyes have all the seeming of a demon's that is dreaming!"

Whoa.

Chapter Four

Whoever had said the demon line had an old-fashioned way of speaking. But the words fit Varken. His sunken, bleary eyes did look like those of a demon. A demon dreaming up evil plans.

It turned out to be a *what*, not a *who*, that was speaking. From the branch of a fake tree a metal raven chirped, "*And my soul from out that shadow that lies floating on the floor/Shall be lifted—nevermore!*"

From the other side of the display I heard loud, forceful footsteps. Varken yanked the bird from its fake nest. Then he ripped away the nest, revealing a speaker.

A wire ran from the speaker down behind the tree. Varken grabbed at the wire. As he struggled to detach it, a fresh round of words burst out:

"*Once upon a midnight dreary*—"

At that point Varken wrenched the wire loose. The frayed end of the wire sizzled, sending off sparks.

That's when Varken spotted Pree. Dropping the still-sizzling wire, he ground his heel into it.

Then, holding the raven high, he stomped up to her.

"I am the display manager. This does not belong in the display. It has nothing to do with 'The Pit and the Pendulum.'"

Pree's eyes widened. "I know that, sir. The raven is from Edgar Allan Poe's poem 'The Raven.' But we ran out of 'Pit and the Pendulum' stuff, and there was still this one display area to fill. So I found a locker full of 'Raven' props. You did tell me I should go ahead and arrange the displays and not bother you."

Varken's glare grew deadlier. Pree didn't notice. As usual, she was getting carried away with her enthusiasm. "'The Raven' is such a great poem, Mr. Varken. It's about a guy who can't get over the loss of his girlfriend. He wants to see her so badly. But this raven shows up and keeps croaking '*Nevermore!*' Sort of chilling in an enjoyable way, if you know what I mean."

Varken gritted his teeth at this outpouring of yakkity-yaks. But I liked them. For the first time I wasn't finding Pree's blathering the slightest bit annoying.

Varken hissed, "I don't allow mistakes, missy. *You're fired.*"

Pree gasped.

Varken stretched out his arm to point Pree toward the exit. The loud *creak!* from his elbow joint echoed in the shocked silence.

"Hey, Varken," I said, trying to sound bold. "You can't fire someone for bringing out the wrong prop. If the raven doesn't belong in the display, why is it here at the Pendulum in the first place?"

In the dim light Varken hadn't seen me standing behind Pree. Startled, he drew back.

I walked up to him. I shoved my face close to his. "You're the manager. You're responsible for what comes into the Pendulum."

Varken still held the raven high. He flexed his bony fingers around it, like he wouldn't mind smashing it down on my head.

"Get out of here, Marlowe. And take your out-of-a-job girlfriend with you."

The raven's eyes glittered at me like a warning. Something was wrong here. Earlier Varken had said he didn't know my name, didn't want to.

He had just spoken it.

Which meant—

He hadn't just happened to see me through the Cliff Edge window. Hadn't just happened to meet me outside the Pendulum.

He knew about me—who I was, that I climbed, that I took my breaks at the amusement park.

But how?

Forget "The Raven." This was chilling—and not in an enjoyable way at all.

But I couldn't stop to figure it out now. In a low voice Pree was saying, "It's okay, Conor. I'll go."

I understood how she felt. It must be embarrassing to have people gawk while you got fired. But I also knew how much this job meant to Pree. This job was going to be her big start.

Varken took out his cell phone as all three of us walked toward the tunnel entrance. He started punching in numbers. "Security?" he barked.

No doubt he was planning to get Pree escorted out of the park. Even more people would gawk at her. Huge crowds of them.

I complained about Pree, sure—in the privacy of my brain. But someone else complaining about her, and out loud? Nope. Not going to happen.

I grabbed his phone from him. I said into it, "Extra large with double cheese—hold the mushrooms."

I clicked the phone off and shoved it against Varken's chest. I said, "Prisha stays. Or I don't make the climb."

Varken was so mad he was white-knuckling the raven. I didn't think he would actually use it as a weapon. Still...

Quick as a ninja, I grabbed the bird from him. Varken was left gaping at his empty hands.

"Now you see it, now you don't," I said.

I picked up the wire and wound it around my shoulder for easy carrying.

"We'll return the raven to the storage room," Pree assured Varken.

"Yeah, we'll make sure it's *safe*," I added. I was happy that now he couldn't use it to clock me upside the head. But something told me the raven was important to him for other reasons. Maybe it was the way his eyes were bugging out.

Now they rolled from Pree to me and back again like out-of-control marbles. He knew I had him. If he didn't keep Pree on, I wouldn't make the climb. He also knew there was nothing, zippo, he could do about it.

A woman pushed through to the front of the crowd forming at the entrance of the tunnel. "Is it true that Edgar Allan Poe was never happy, not one day of his life?" she asked.

"How should I know?" Varken snapped.

"He was only forty when he died. I can't stand to think he spent every minute of those forty years unhappy!" the woman added.

"My own life is wasting away right now," Varken growled.

"How rude!"

Pree and I took advantage of the distraction to head to the storage room.

As we walked I shifted the raven from one hand to the other. I realized it wasn't made of metal. It was carved out of a hard, dark wood. Ebony maybe. Even in the dim light its burnished surface gave off a reddish glow.

The bird's eyes sparkled up at me like it was alive. Like it had a joke it wanted to share.

A critter like you should be in an art gallery, not jammed in a locker with props, I thought.

Once we were out of Varken's sight, Pree stopped and turned to me. Her eyes shone. "Thank you for saving my job, Conor."

I shrugged. I didn't feel like talking about it. Not that I had regrets about saving her job. But now I had committed to Varken. Now I had to do the climb.

"You guys only wanted Pendulum props. So how did the raven get here?" I asked, to change the subject.

"Professor Pennyfeather sent us a bunch of 'Raven' things by accident."

It was hard to hear. We were near the door where people filed out to the ride. Everybody was gabbing excitedly.

"Penny what?" I asked,

"Penny*feather*. He's a famous Edgar Allan Poe scholar. The hundred and seventieth anniversary of Edgar Allan's death is coming up this year. The university is planning a special exhibit. Professor Pennyfeather, who's in charge of the exhibit, has collected a lot of stuff in preparation.

"The prof has phoned Varken several times. He's upset about his mistake. Tomorrow he's sending somebody to pick up the 'Raven' locker." Pree sighed.

"I didn't think there was any harm in displaying the props today. The little guy is so cute!"

The raven's eyes twinkled at her like he understood.

We walked on. Now we were by the door. We saw the Pendulum's big, gleaming, crescent-shaped car waiting beside the ride platform.

On the platform an attendant waved people forward, two at a time. He helped them in. He handed each person a barf bag.

Whenever I'd gone on the ride, it had been Varken handing out the bags. This new guy must be the other student they had hired.

But he wasn't just any guy. He was Bull Bakker.

Yeah, that Bull. The big, hulking guy I had jeered at all those years ago. The guy I had spent so much time running away from in elementary school.

Bull squinted at the doorway, saw me.

He glowered.

Ah, yes. That I'm-going-to-smash-your-teeth-out-the-back-of-your-head expression. I remembered it well.

Clenching his fists, Bull lumbered toward me.

Chapter Five

He couldn't help it. It was force of habit.

"What, you're just leaving your customers?" I called.

It was sweltering in the hot sun. People were getting cranky. "Hey, Incredible Hulk!" one guy shouted. "Get back here!"

Bull glared at me but went back to helping people onto the ride.

He didn't stay quiet though. After settling in an old lady, he pointed the barf bag at me. "I've told people about you, Conor Marlowe. How you think you're so great with your climbing."

I held up the thick mass of wires I'd wound into a circle. I made like I was about to throw them. "Hey, Bull. Stand still and I'll use you for ring toss."

"Know what, Marlowe? *Monkeys* climb." Curling his arms at his sides, Bull moved his fists up and down. "Oo-oo, aw-aw, ee-ee!"

"*Conor*." Pree glared at me from the walkway.

Right. No time for immaturity. I hefted the circle of wires back up on my shoulder. I followed her down the tunnel.

Not that I didn't enjoy being immature. Immaturity is one of life's little pleasures.

But I had just realized something that took the fun out of it.

I've told people about you, Conor Marlowe.

Bull Bakker. That's how Varken had found out about me.

The storage room was at the end of the walkway. Pree unlocked the door.

A row of lockers stretched across the room. Each locker bore the painted words *Professor Pennyfeather's Poe Props*.

Wow. Try saying that out loud fast.

Pree fixed a solemn gaze on me. "What is this climb you're doing for Varken? Is it dangerous?"

Varken's gray face floated into my brain. *I have a package for you to hide... a secret...*

Secret meant illegal. I couldn't get Pree mixed up in this.

I tried to make a joke of it. I spun the end of an invisible mustache. "Young woman, nothing is dangerous for the one, the only, Climbing Fiend."

With a huff, Pree turned away. She went down the row of lockers, checking inside each one. She stopped. "Okay, this is the Raven locker."

She opened the door wide. A skeleton grinned out at us. It sported long false eyelashes, a red-lipsticked mouth and a wig of brown hair.

"Yikes," I said.

Pree giggled. "Meet Lenore. She's the dead girl in the poem, the one the speaker keeps calling out for. The raven keeps telling him '*Nevermore!*' But the guy can't accept her death. He can't let go."

Wedged at the back of the locker was a painting of a sad-faced man with unruly dark hair.

"That's Edgar Allan Poe," Pree explained. "He based the grieving guy in 'The Raven' on himself. Edgar Allan couldn't get over the death of his wife."

I leaned in for a closer look. The haunted eyes in the painting seemed to be begging for relief from his misery.

Or at least for one good belly laugh.

"Forty years, all of them unhappy," I said.

"Poor guy," sighed Pree.

Turned out Pree wasn't the only one who agreed with me.

Lenore was nodding vigorously. *What?*

Turned out, by leaning in I had nudged the skeleton off balance.

Lenore creaked and swayed. Her wig slipped partway off her head. She lurched out at us.

Pree and I pushed her back in. The movement was too much for the fragile skeleton. Her right hand broke off and fell to the floor.

I really did not want to touch it. But Pree was frantically trying to prop the rest of Lenore against the painting so there wouldn't be any more tumbles. It was up to me to grab the hand.

I reached down, forced myself to grasp it. It was heavier than I'd expected. I turned it palm up. A short, fat white candle was stuck to the palm. With that extra weight, no surprise the hand had come loose.

The locker had a built-in shelf. I set Lenore's hand on it.

An empty cloth bag also lay on the shelf. A label on the side read *Raven*.

This was where my sparkly-eyed buddy should go.

I was still holding the raven. I looked down at it. I had an absurd impulse to apologize. I mean, I wouldn't want to be shut up with that grinning, crooked-wigged skeleton.

Sssh...sssh...

Pree and I exchanged glances. We recognized that shuffling sound.

Varken was in the storage room.

"What's taking you so long, missy?" he bellowed. "You fooling around with that boyfriend of yours?"

Pree blushed. I grinned. How could I have ever found Pree annoying? As of today I liked her. A lot.

"Care to fool around?" I whispered.

She blushed deeper. I grinned wider.

Then I caught Lenore's eye. Or, rather, Lenore's eyeless socket.

Talk about a mood ruiner.

"We're just putting the raven away," I called.

I looked from the raven to the bag on the shelf. I thought how claustrophobic it would feel to be tied up in a bag.

But that was dumb. The bird wasn't real. It couldn't feel.

Varken appeared at the end of the row of lockers.

"Put the bird away, Marlowe," he snarled. "Then get out of here."

I reached into the locker. The bag was just beyond Lenore's hand. My fingers brushed her cold, bony ones.

I flinched. I reminded myself her hand was lifeless. Therefore harmless.

I got hold of the bag. I avoided knocking against the rest of Lenore.

That didn't stop the old girl from sharing her opinion.

Blood-curdling yells rang out from the locker.

Chapter Six

I jumped back. "The yelling came from her! I even saw that lipsticked mouth move."

It sounded stupid and crazy. It *was* stupid and crazy. But Pree and Varken had heard it too. And the fear in my voice. They peered in at Lenore.

My heart was thudding. I had to calm down.

You're a climber, Marlowe. So do what climbers do. Get a grip.

I felt in my jacket pocket. Pulling out a leftover paper napkin from lunch, I wiped my forehead with it.

Pree and Varken stepped back from the locker. Pree said uncertainly, "Many of these props are mechanized. You must have accidentally pressed a button."

I shrugged. I was tying the strings of the bag into double and triple knots. I spotted some duct tape on top of one of the lockers. Grabbing it, I tore a long strip off with my teeth. I wound it around the bag several times over. To keep the bag secure.

And to hide the fact that my hands were shaking.

I held the bag up. I wagged it at Varken, tick-tock. "Satisfied?"

Varken's nicotine-yellow fingers closed around the bag. He set it on the locker shelf, then slammed the door shut. Like the mysterious yelling, the slam echoed several times over.

I shoved my hands into my jacket pockets. I sniffed the air. "Hey, Varken. You smoke in here? Your bosses might have something to say about breaking the no-smoking rules."

It was a wild shot. In reality, the fumes coming off Varken were so strong I couldn't tell if they were from a recent smoke break in the storage room. He just reeked.

But Varken winced. I had guessed right about him sneaking in here.

Brushing past us, he stomped out of the storage room—no doubt to calm himself with a cigarette outside the park fence.

When he was gone, I said, "I could report Varken and his disgusting habit to management. They might bring in another manager. Someone halfway sane."

Pree shook her head. "He'd just deny it. He'd say it was a cleaner who lit up in here. They'd believe him. Varken used to be an actor. He's a good one when he wants to be."

I thought of how complimentary Varken had been when he'd first approached me. How he'd pretended not to know who I was.

I nodded. "He can act all right. I bet he had a nice run of goblin roles—no need for makeup."

That, at least, got a wry smile out of Pree. "Now he's my own personal goblin. Well, I better get back to work before the goblin gets even madder at me. I have to fill that empty space in the display. Maybe I can move some dummy prison guards into it."

"I could help," I offered. "But if

Varken spotted me, I'm not sure I'd be doing you any favors."

She smiled at me. A radiant smile this time. "That's okay. You made it possible for me to keep coming here every day. Thanks again, Conor."

I ran, or possibly floated, through the tunnel. The mechanical rat could have chomped a chunk out of my scalp and I wouldn't have noticed.

All I could think of was Pree's radiant smile. She liked me!

I passed the door to the ride. From the platform Bull Bakker glowered at me.

Glowering I could take. Blabbing I didn't like.

I brushed by the people lined up for the Pendulum.

"You told Varken about me," I said, pointing a finger at his chest. "Maybe you should live your own life instead of talking about mine to everyone you meet. You are such a *loser*."

Bull drew back. He looked...hurt. I suddenly realized that even bulls could be human.

I realized something else too. I wasn't being fair.

No question it was Bull who had told Varken about me. Varken had then waited and watched for me. Sure of my stupid confidence, the old crook had pounced. *Think you could climb it?*

But *I* was the one, not Bull, who had agreed to Varken's crazy plan.

The loser here was me.

"Maybe I was a bit hasty just now," I said to Bull.

But I didn't know if Bull had heard. People were shouting.

"Hey, Hulk Hogan! Why are you letting that guy butt into the front of the line?"

Grabbing my shoulders, Bull easily lifted me off the ground. His grip tightened. He began crushing my shoulder bones.

The Bullster was finally going to get his revenge for all the cracks I'd made about him.

He was about to crack *me*—into walnut-size pieces.

Chapter Seven

But it wasn't the splintering of bones I felt. It was a rush of sunny air.

I was falling.

I landed, more or less sitting up, in a Pendulum seat. Bull had thrown me into the ride.

I stood up. *Ow.* I started to climb out. "Okay, Bull. You got even with me and my big mouth. Now let me take my battered bones and get out of here."

Bull scowled. "This has nothing to do with getting even, Marlowe. I need you to stay still. Act like everything is normal. If Varken sees trouble in the lineup, he will fire me."

These were the most words Bull had ever said to me. Up till now our conversation had been on the minimal side—I wisecracked, he roared and chased me up a tree.

I noticed how carefully Bull was speaking. His first language was not English. He was Dutch. He and his family had moved here from Amsterdam.

Just then Varken poked his head through the doorway. He squinted around, making sure everything was running smoothly.

I scrunched down in my seat. Bull looked at me. His scowl faded.

He nodded. With Varken as a common enemy, our relationship had thawed. Not a lot. From ice cold to lukewarm maybe. But still.

People from the lineup piled into the rest of the seats. Bull checked everyone, locking them in with the safety clamps.

A sign on the back of each seat read *Keep hold of your possessions—they could go flying!* I shoved my hands in my pockets to stop anything from falling out.

The woman beside me was holding an e-reader. She set it on her lap so she could tuck her hair up into her ballcap. The title page of the book she was reading beamed up at me: *Ravin' About Raven*, by Professor Hugh Pennyfeather.

Pennyfeather! The guy who had sent the Raven locker here by mistake.

The woman noticed me looking at the e-reader. "According to this book," she said, "Poe had a secret that he wouldn't tell anyone. I wonder what it could be."

I was more concerned about her e-reader. "Ma'am, we're about ready for takeoff. Maybe you should hang on to that."

The woman laughed. "I'm not worried about you stealing it!"

"That's not what I—"

Tick... The crescent-shaped car swung sideways. This first swing was a gentle one. The Pendulum version of, say, a Sunday drive with the folks.

Tock... The next swing, up in the opposite direction, was a bit longer and higher. Still Sunday-drive-ish.

The woman fiddled with her ballcap again.

Wham! The Pendulum wrenched us wa-a-a-a-ay up to the other side. The e-reader flew off the woman's lap. For an instant it glittered in the sun. Then—

It landed on the platform with a smash.

The woman screamed. Most other people were screaming too. I kept my hands in my pockets and gritted my teeth. I pressed my back hard against the seat to try to keep from lurching.

I was kind of enjoying myself.

The Pendulum hurled us higher. The air whipped our faces. It chest-punched the oxygen out of us.

The car sliced up through the sky. It felt like we were about to be flung into outer space.

I had been on the ride before, so I knew that wouldn't happen. But for a second there it sure felt like it would.

I also knew this was the Pendulum's final throw. The killer finale.

The car swung lower, and the ticking slowed. As we reached the platform, the ominous *tick...tock...*stopped.

The quiet was sweet.

It didn't last long.

The woman gave a shriek. She pointed at her battered e-reader.

She started climbing out of the car.

Too late. Tucking the last of a donut into his mouth, Bull hurried along the platform to help people out of the cars.

What can I say? He is a big guy with big feet. And he was in a big hurry.

His right foot bashed down on the device.

The woman looked at me in horror. "Oh no! Do you think it's—"

I shrugged. Maybe a joke would make her feel better. "Like the bird says in the poem, '*Nevermore*...'"

Knowing I had to be back at the park by two AM, I tried to catch some z's after dinner. They weren't great z's. Uneasy ones. I dreamed that a skeleton's hand was reaching over my windowsill.

The broken-off hand waved at me. It started scratching at the sill.

I woke up. Wind was scraping leaves against the windowpane.

I checked my phone. The alarm was just about to go off so I got up. I had slept in my clothes. I was ready to go and get this over with.

I picked up the Cliff Edge windbreaker I had been wearing earlier. The edge of the paper napkin still stuck out of one pocket.

The night felt too cold for a windbreaker. I rolled it into a ball and stuck it at the back of my drawer. No one could say I didn't put my clothes away.

I slipped on a heavier jacket. In the back pocket of my jeans I still had the wad of money. I would give it back to Varken tonight. There had been too many people around earlier. I was doing the climb to save Pree's job, but I didn't want any other ties to Varken. The guy was way too shifty for my liking.

I climbed out the window to the tree outside. I dropped lightly from branch to branch, then down to the lawn.

I started jogging. I reached the highway. The park was up ahead. The lights of the now-still rides glowed against the dark sky.

Near the gate a figure stood in the shadows. Varken?

I jogged closer. I could tell now that it was too big to be Varken.

The figure lumbered out of the shadows.

"Bull Bakker," I said.

I wasn't nervous. Today things had changed. We now realized we had an enemy in common. We'd bonded. Heck, you might even say we were fr—

Bull raised a long stick over his head.

The moonlight lit it up. Not a stick. A spear.

He was aiming it at my heart.

Chapter Eight

All because I had laughed at him all those years ago? He couldn't be serious.

Still, I stepped back.

Something crackled underfoot. I glanced down. A chocolate-bar wrapper.

I stared at Bull, at the spear he held high above his head.

Sure, he could be a vengeful warrior out for blood revenge.

Or…

I picked up the wrapper. I jumped up and spiked the wrapper on the point of the spear.

"So you work at the Pendulum by day and clean up garbage by night," I said. "Two jobs. You must be pulling in a lot of money."

Bull grunted. "The regular garbage guy is sick. I am filling in for him. I do that sometimes for extra money."

"That's awesome," I said. I meant it. I was relieved the spear wasn't a possible murder weapon.

Bull nodded. This was good. We were making progress.

Or so I thought.

Bull gave a sharp gasp. He dropped his spear.

He was staring past me. I turned.

Victor Varken was at the park gate. His fingers curled around the rails like claws. His teeth were bared.

Grabbing the spear again, Bull rushed past Varken and through the gate.

It was my turn to stare at the Pendulum manager. I got that Varken was a tough boss. I knew Pree was scared of him.

But for *Bull* to be that frightened? I didn't get it.

"What have you done to Bull Bakker?" I demanded.

Varken snapped, "Mind your own business, climbing boy."

He was carrying a briefcase. He slammed it into my ribs, prodding me through the gates.

Always the charmer.

We walked up to the Pendulum. The big, gleaming blade looked like a crescent moon that had fallen from the sky.

Varken led me to one of the vertical bars. It had footholds going all the way up. For maintenance types doing checks or repairs, I guessed.

Or stupid-confident teenagers making illegal climbs.

Varken pulled out the duct-taped cloth bag from his briefcase. He glanced around. No one was watching. He shoved it into my hands.

"Listen up. At the top you'll find a supplies box. Open it. Stash the bag inside. Then come back down and scram."

His cigarette-fumed breath stank up the air. I stepped back. I wanted to shove the bag at him, run away. Let him do the climb.

I pictured Varken struggling up the holds. One of his coughing fits would strike. His grip on the holds would weaken, slip. He'd fall.

Varken rasped, "What, you waiting for old-age pension to kick in? The guard will be back to patrol this area in twenty minutes. You have to make the climb now."

I gazed up. It was a clear night. The stars blazed up and up into the sky—like wall holds, I thought.

I imagined climbing them. I'd just keep going, right into outer space.

Now that would be the *real* forever sky.

Okay, so it was impossible.

But the horizontal bar—that was possible. That I could reach.

I had to climb it. For Pree. Otherwise Varken would fire her.

Besides, I now wanted to make the climb. I wanted to reach the top of the tower, get closer to that starry sky.

Hogg was right about me. I was stupid-confident.

I recognized that.

Cramming the cloth bag into my back-pack, I started the climb.

It started out like all climbs. At first I was ultra-aware of my weight, of gravity pulling at me.

I concentrated on gripping the holds, on keeping each foot and hand movement the same. If you're right-handed, you're tempted to throw your right hand up in a big, fast movement. You're less confident about your left hand. Your instinct is to reach with your left hand in a small, careful movement. But you can't do that. You have to find total balance.

I found that balance. I got into the pace, the rhythm, of the climb. I lightened up. I became motion, not weight.

I got to the horizontal bar. I stood. I tipped my head back and looked at the stars. This was it. This was what I climbed for. Man, talk about the perfect moment—

I heard a voice.

I looked down.

Varken had got the security guard's schedule wrong. The guard wasn't patrolling the other side of the park. He was walking up to Varken, ready for a chat.

Ready at any moment to glance up—and see me.

Chapter Nine

I froze. What had I been thinking? This wasn't the perfect moment. Just the opposite. I was *trespassing*. If the guard saw me, he would call the cops. I'd be busted.

I doubted there was a way to climb out of juvie court.

I cursed myself for being so arrogant. I thought of Hogg shaking his head and rolling his eyes. He knew me better than I did.

Varken clapped an arm around the guard's shoulders. I couldn't hear what they were saying, but I could tell that Varken was leading the guard toward the tunnel.

As Varken had said, a metal supply box sat on the horizontal bar. Kind of coffin-shaped. Edgar Allan would have approved.

I unfastened the latch, lifted the lid. I pulled the bag from my backpack.

I thought of the raven, of the way its eyes shone. Of its smooth ebony that glinted red in the light.

I stashed the bag in the supply box. I hoped I was doing the right thing. I didn't like the thought of the raven being cooped up. But at least it was safe.

I shut the lid.

As I climbed down, Varken jabbed

his forefinger up at me. I figured he'd distracted the guard.

"You planning to hang a coat on that?" I called.

I was only about five feet off the ground. I decided not to take the footholds the rest of the way down. That jabby finger could poke an eye out. Instead I jumped sideways.

Varken fumed. "Don't get funny with me, climbing boy. Did you hide the bag like I told you? Because if you didn't hide it, if you just pretended to, I'll find out."

I stared at his finger, white and bony in the night air. It reminded me of the skeleton's broken-off hand.

I pulled my jacket pockets inside out. I showed him the inside of my backpack. No raven.

Varken bared his yellow teeth at me. "Fine. We're done, you and I. We don't know each other. Now get out."

He shuffled off.

I stared at his bent, retreating figure. *If you didn't hide it, I'll find out*. But how would he find out? It's not like *he* would climb the Pendulum.

I thought of something else too. Varken wasn't going to leave his precious package up there forever. One day he'd want it back.

He would get somebody else to climb. Some other stupid-confident kid.

Maybe he'd force Bull to do it. Bull seemed scared enough of Varken to do anything. Where had Bull gone, anyway?

I tucked my jacket pockets back in. Then I remembered. They were empty—but my jeans pocket wasn't.

I still had to return Varken's money.

"Wait!" I shouted.

It was no use. Varken didn't hear me. He was on his cell phone. I watched him disappear around the roller coaster.

I ran after him.

On the other side of the coaster was a long white trailer marked *PARK EMPLOYEES ONLY*.

The lights were on in the trailer. I got up close. Through an open window I could see Bull at a counter. He was clanking a spoon in a steaming mug. The scent of chocolate drifted out.

So did Bull's voice. Earbuds in, he was singing along to a song. "*Teenager in lo-o-ove*," he crooned.

Oka-a-ay.

I spotted Varken on the other side of the trailer, over by the fence. He was still jabbering on his phone.

He was also smoking, taking deep, shuddery drags off his cigarette. Every few seconds he blew the smoke through the chain links, toward the highway.

I guess for Varken this qualified as not smoking inside the park.

I walked toward him. He didn't see me.

I got close enough to hear what he was saying.

"I'll keep the climbing kid quiet, all right. Quiet as death."

Chapter Ten

Varken broke into cackles of laughter.

Varken was planning to…kill me?

The idea of that cough-wracked smoker taking me on made me mad, not scared. I'd like to see him try. I'd squash him.

I ducked into the long shadows of the roller coaster so I could keep listening.

As usual, Varken's cackles turned into coughs. He spat through a link. The stream of spit went right through without catching on the fence.

Impressive aim. The guy would be great at parties.

He snapped, "Okay, bro. No need to fall out of that wheelchair of yours. I won't do anything to the kid."

So it was Varken's brother on the other end. Correction. Wheelchair-bound brother.

Just two health-challenged seniors having a friendly chat—

About murder.

Whatever happened to bridge games and lawn bowling?

Varken blew a fresh cloud of smoke through the chain links. "Anyhow, we got nothing to worry about. Marlowe's sweet on this girl who works for me. He messes with me, the girl gets fired."

Varken lit a fresh cigarette. “Here’s how it’s going to work. Pennyfeather will send a truck for his Raven locker. The truck gets back, the prof sees the raven is missing. He asks me about it. I act clueless. I deny even looking inside the locker. Say it was the Pendulum stuff I was interested in.”

Varken lowered his voice. I had to strain to hear him.

“You and I will wait a while…cash the raven in…I find a beach somewhere.”

Then he barked with laughter and forgot to muffle his voice. “You can join me, brother dear. Except your wheels might get stuck in the sand!”

Varken laughed himself into another coughing fit.

What a guy, making fun of his brother’s disability.

Bull came out of the trailer just as Varken reached the steps. Bull’s eyes widened. He tried to speak but choked on his words.

"Get out of my way," Varken snarled.

Bull gulped. He stepped back and stumbled onto the grass.

Varken tossed his cigarette butt sideways and stomped inside the trailer.

Whoa. The still-lit butt was flying straight at me.

I ducked before it sizzled my face or possibly an eyeball.

With my running shoe I ground the butt out on the grass. I considered giving Varken a little lecture on fire hazards.

A lecture might not be all I'd give him. I was mad enough about his little death joke to punch his face in.

But I didn't want Varken to know I'd overheard him just now. I needed to get away and think about what to do next.

Bull was still standing there but hadn't spotted me. If he hadn't blabbed about me to Varken, I wouldn't be in this mess. But still I felt sorry for him. Imagine having a boss who scared you like that!

Staying in the shadows, I crept back around the roller coaster and headed home.

I climbed up the tree and into my bedroom. It was still dark. Maybe I could get some sleep.

Except that my brain wouldn't let me.

Tick...

Varken would spin a tale to Professor Pennyfeather. During the trip to the amusement park the raven had fallen out. Now it was missing. Things like that happened all the time with deliveries.

Tock...

Varken planned to sell it. The ebony bird with the sparkly eyes was his retirement fund.

Well, tick, tock, Varken was in for a shock. I was going to get the bird back to Pennyfeather.

After all, I knew where it was.

It got light outside. I heard my folks downstairs, leaving for work.

I swung out of bed. I did some stretching exercises. They made me feel better. Now I knew what I had to do. Go to the police. Tell them everything.

I did some running on the spot. I wondered what made the raven so valuable that Varken could retire off it. The bird must be an antique. Maybe it had belonged to Edgar Allan Poe. Maybe he had kept it on his desk for good luck.

But Poe's writing was all about bad luck. It reflected his gloomy life.

I remembered the lady at the Pendulum displays. *Is it true Edgar Allan Poe was never happy, not one day of his life?*

I hoped it wasn't true. I mean, not even one happy day? Sheesh.

It was time to get moving. Stretching had cleared my brain. Now I needed to shock it into action. Jumping into the shower, I turned the water up to near scalding.

Again I thought about what a mess I'd gotten into. Like Hogg always said, stupid-confident.

I switched the water off and stood there, steam roiling around me, water dripping into my eyes. Hogg. That was it. My boss mentored me, encouraged me, put up with me. First of all I'd talk to Hogg. It would be good to get some things off my chest, get calm before going to the police.

I felt better just thinking about it.

Hogg was leaning back in his chair, feet up on his desk. He was eating his usual breakfast—nuts and dried berries out of a cereal box.

He held out the box. "Help yourself."

"Actually, I need to talk to you about something. A problem."

Hogg rolled the chair closer and fixed me with his piercing blue eyes. "Yeah, you have a problem, Marlowe. You look ragged. That's not good. A climber needs to clock in eight hours' sleep minimum."

I shrugged. "Bad night."

Hogg sat back. He shook his head and sighed. But his face was kind. "So speak."

"I met this crazy—" I stopped. I had been about to say *old man*. But Hogg was in his early sixties. He might take offense.

"Crazy person," I said instead.

I looked out the window at the amusement park. The fair hadn't opened yet. The Pendulum sat still, the huge, crescent-shaped blade glowing in the sun.

But it was something a lot closer that caught my gaze.

Another old man, scowling through the Cliff Edge window at me.

An old man in a wheelchair.

Varken's brother. It had to be.

Chapter Eleven

The lack of sleep was getting to me. The guy scowling through the glass didn't have to be Varken's brother. He could just be a passerby.

A passerby in a wheelchair stopping by a climbing studio?

Hogg got up to see who I was staring at. "Friend of yours?"

I went to the door, opened it. "What do you want?"

The guy seemed taken aback. If he was just a passerby, he was probably thinking I was pretty rude.

"I'm betting you're Conor Marlowe," he said. "A mutual friend told me about a little favor you are doing, a certain climbing project." He smiled like we were buddies in on a secret together.

I didn't smile back. I didn't want to be buddies with him.

He leaned forward in his wheelchair. "I wanted to check in with you. Make sure everything was okay."

"I have nothing to say."

His smile faded. He studied me. "And you plan to keep it that way, saying nothing?"

A threat hung over his words—like the Pendulum blade over its victim I couldn't help thinking.

I shook off the thought. The guy was trying to scare me. Well, I wouldn't let him. What could the Varken brothers do to me? They were just two frail old men.

I said, "Get out of here or I'll call the police."

"Police!" The old man reached into the inside pocket of his jacket.

Maybe he kept mints in that inside pocket. That's what people often reached for. Nice to freshen up your breath while chatting.

But now that I looked, it was an L-shaped bulge in that jacket pocket.

A jumbo pack of breath mints?

I didn't think so.

I practically dived back inside Cliff Edge. I locked the door.

"You need to call the police," I told Hogg. "The guy at the door has a gun."

Hogg strode over to the window. He looked out. He barked with laughter.

"That guy wheeling down the sidewalk? Marlowe, you really need to get some sleep."

I looked out the window again. Varken's brother was making his way to the highway. I noticed him adjusting something on the side of his chair. Maybe shifting into a lower gear for going down the hill. He rolled out of view. I stared at the spot where he had been. Maybe I had imagined the gun.

I followed Hogg back to his desk. He sat down, put his feet back up. "Now tell me what's going on."

I nodded. "The manager of the Pendulum got me mixed up in a theft," I said. I looked down at the floor. "He suckered me into climbing the Pendulum and hiding a package. Because, just like you said, I'm stupid-confident."

Hogg sat up, obviously surprised.

I hated telling him I was part of a crime. But I made myself look him in the eye. "It's not just the manager who's involved. His brother's in it too. That guy who was just here."

Hogg frowned. "Tell me more."

I took another deep breath. I said, "They needed me to make the climb. Varken is too weak. He'd fall. And his brother—well, he's in a..."

Wheelchair, I was about to say.

But then, because I was speaking in such a low voice, Hogg moved closer to hear me better.

That is, he rolled closer on the wheels of his office chair.

Chairs, I thought numbly. Chairs with wheels.

Chairs with wheels didn't have to be wheelchairs. They could be *office* chairs.

In that case, Varken's joke about wheels getting stuck wouldn't be cruel. It would be a way of teasing someone who liked to spin and roll his office chair around like he was in the Indy 500.

Someone like Hogg.

"Marlowe?" Hogg was getting impatient.

Someone like Hogg.

Like Hogg, but not Hogg. Of course not. Hogg couldn't be Varken's brother. For one thing, their last names were different.

Right. It was impossible. I shut my brain down against the idea. Over. Done with.

Except...

Hogg knows you. He knows you're stupid-confident. He could be the one who told Varken about you.

No. It was Bull Bakker who had told Varken about me. I was sure of it. Just yesterday Bull had bragged about telling everyone how arrogant I was.

Unless Bull had been bluffing.

Hogg sighed. "Marlowe! You waiting for old-age pension to kick in?"

I stared at him. But it was Varken I was hearing. Urging me to hurry up and climb the Pendulum.

Okay, so Hogg and Varken had an expression in common. That didn't mean they were brothers.

Hogg's bright blue eyes stared back at me. Bright blue like a summer sky. No one with eyes like that could be dishonest.

Then, for an instant, Hogg's face wavered. It changed into the thin, gray, bleary-eyed face of Varken.

I blinked my eyes. Hogg's face reappeared.

Man, I definitely needed more sleep.

Either that—

Or I was onto something.

I blurted, "I'll have to get back to you, sir. I need to speak to a friend."

"C'mon, kid. I'm your friend. You can talk to me."

I wiped my forehead on the sleeve of my Cliff Edge T-shirt. I wanted so badly to believe Hogg. I wanted to tell him everything.

I couldn't though. Not yet. I had to be smart for a change, not stupid-confident. I had to think things out. Play it right.

Chapter Twelve

I found Bull on his porch. He was snoring in a hammock.

"Bull."

He kept snoring. He was still in his maintenance uniform.

I took out my bottle of water. Unscrewing the top, I emptied half the bottle on Bull's face.

He jumped up and rolled out of the hammock, clenching his fists. “Marlowe! This time I’m gonna get you.”

Normally at this point I would scale the nearest tree. But I needed information from Bull, and fast.

“You said you went around telling people about me. About my climbing, how I think I’m so great. Was Varken one of the people you told?”

The rage on Bull’s face faded. He looked sheepish. “I don’t go around talking about you. I was only making that up. I was messing with you like you mess with me.”

I nodded. “I guess we’ve wasted a lot of time messing with each other.”

Bull muttered, “I only pretend to make fun of your climbing. I wish I could climb like you. But I’m too big. My weight drags me down.”

I balanced the water bottle on my palm. "Climbing's got nothing to do with size or weight, Bull. It's about balance. See this bottle? It stays where it is because it's balanced, not because it's light."

I moved my palm around. The bottle swayed but didn't fall. "I'll show you how to climb if you want."

Bull spluttered. Maybe he was trying to thank me. But was too stunned to get the words out.

This could go on for hours. I held up my hand to stop him. "You have to do me a favor first. Tell me why you're afraid of Varken."

His eyes bulged. "I—I can't. I promised."

"Promises to slimeballs don't count."

He breathed heavily in and out, thinking about this.

I dropped the bottle in my backpack. I made like I was ready to leave.

"Wait." Bull stepped in front of me, blocking my way down the porch steps. He hesitated.. "I promised to keep quiet about—about—"

He coughed. His face looked like it usually did when he was around Varken.

Amazing how just the mention of Varken got him terrified.

He choked. His face grew scarlet. I wondered if I should call 9-1-1.

Then—

Bull burst into laughter. Finally he gasped out, "*Varken* is the Dutch word for *hog*!"

"Hog," I repeated slowly. "Like the animal. Or like a last name that somebody would tack on an extra *g* to. Make it look different than plain, barnyard *hog*."

Bull nodded. "Varken told me his great-grandfather came over from Holland. Great-grandpa decided a more English-sounding name would help him succeed. So he translated *Varken* into *Hog*. He added the extra *g,* like you say, to fancy it up."

I now knew Varken and Hogg were brothers. One thing I didn't get though. "So why did Varken change his last name back to the Dutch?"

"I asked him that. He changed it when he was a young guy starting out in acting. He said no one would give handsome-leading-man roles to a guy named Hogg."

Gray, bent, cough-racked Varken… handsome? I had assumed he'd played only horror roles.

Curious, I took out my phone and looked up Victor Varken on the International Movie Database.

A young blond man with dazzling white teeth smiled out at me, along with a list of roles in old TV shows.

It was like looking at a photo of my boss when he was thirty years younger.

But Hogg had stayed healthy. He'd kept his good looks. Varken could have kept his too, but for his killer smoking habit.

Bull explained, "My first day they sent me to work at the Pendulum. When I met Varken I joked, 'So you are a *hog*, sir?'

"Varken didn't like that I knew Dutch. He didn't like being laughed at. He threatened to fire me if I ever mentioned the hog thing again. That made it worse! The harder I tried not to think it, the more I laughed."

I recalled the fear on Bull's face whenever Varken appeared. All those times he had been afraid...that he would burst out laughing.

Bull went back into his house.

I took out my phone.

Hogg picked up on the first ring. "Yeah?"

"Meet me at the top of the Pendulum in an hour."

Silence.

"You remember me. Conor Marlowe. The stupid-confident guy who climbed the Pendulum for you."

"I don't understand."

Sure he did. And I was going to get him to admit it. Then I would go to the police.

"At the top of the...are you *crazy?* I'm not going to climb that thing."

"You'll climb it if you want Edgar Allan Poe's raven," I said and hung up.

Bull came out of his house carrying two cinnamon buns. He offered one to me.

He read my face. "You're going to get Varken."

"I'm going to try."

"He is a bad person." With his slow, careful way of talking, Bull had put it simply and perfectly.

"He's double trouble," I agreed.

I turned. Time for my little meet-and-greet.

Bull chewed thoughtfully on a piece of cinnamon bun. "I will help you."

I paused.

Bull nodded. "Yes. I will help. I don't want to be afraid to laugh."

Tough to argue with that.

Chapter Thirteen

Bull and I arrived at the Pendulum just before the park opened.

Pree came up the walkway. Seeing us, she broke into a wide smile.

I was nervous about my upcoming faceoff with Hogg. But I felt better seeing Pree. What an idiot I'd been all this time not to appreciate her.

"Hi, Bull. What are you doing here, Conor?"

People were filing past us. I wanted to tell Pree how I felt about her right away. But I could hardly do that with others around.

"I'm just checking on something," I told her. "Talk to you later, okay?"

She nodded and started helping Bull take tickets.

I walked through the displays to the ride platform. I looked up the footholds to the horizontal bar, to the sunny blue beyond.

Again I felt nervous. But nervousness couldn't be part of climbing.

I stepped onto the lowest foothold, reached up to grip another. I took the climb slower than usual. I kept every move the same. I made sure each move lasted the same amount of time. All the while I took deep, slow breaths.

I felt myself grow lighter. In getting physically balanced, I felt my mental balance coming back too. The nervousness fell away.

I reached the top of the horizontal bar. I breathed in the clear air. I turned my face up to the sun and closed my eyes. This was good.

I heard soft, evenly spaced footfalls below me. Hogg was climbing the Pendulum.

I took my phone out. I turned on the recording app, then put the phone back in my pocket.

I didn't have much time to get Hogg to talk. Bull was stalling the customers. He was saying the ride would be delayed a few minutes. They'd buy that for just so long. Then they'd start grumbling, followed by yelling and insults.

People who like thrill rides aren't the patient type.

Hogg stepped onto the horizontal bar. I thought he'd be angry. He wasn't. He looked concerned. Maybe acting talent ran in the family.

"You're in some kind of trouble. On the phone you talked about giving me a raven. Why don't you do that? Then we'll figure this whole thing out."

"I can't just hand the raven over. It's not that easy."

"Sure it's easy."

Hogg stepped around me. He was heading to the coffin-shaped supply box.

I had to distract him.

"Wait," I said.

But something else distracted Hogg. A faint *whish*ing from below. Like a breeze. Or a broom sweeping a floor.

Hogg started to look over the side.

I had to get his attention. I needed him to talk. Maybe if I relaxed him, loosened him up.

"Remember the guy who showed up at Cliff Edge in a wheelchair? I was sure he was Victor's brother. Turns out he was just some random guy in a wheelchair."

Hogg shot me an impatient look. He didn't care about the random guy.

Okay, so forget the chatty approach. "Tell me how you and Victor got involved in theft," I blurted.

A smile crooked up one side of Hogg's face. "All right, Marlowe. I owe you an explanation. But it has to be private, just the two of us."

I stared at him. "Am I missing something? It's just the two of us up here."

He shook his head. "Come now. You got me up here to confess. Don't tell me you're not recording everything I say."

"I, uh…"

"You see how well I know you?" Hogg said. "I knew you would accept Victor's challenge and climb the Pendulum. I also knew you might regret it because of your fine young conscience. And now you're trying to get a confession from me so you can turn it over to the police."

His smile broadened. I could guess his thoughts. I was stupid-confident. He was smart.

"Kindly give me your phone."

I handed it over. There was nothing else I could do.

The screen showed my recording app ticking away. Hogg switched the phone off. He placed it on the horizontal bar. "Okay. I'll make this fast. Professor Pennyflubber—"

"Penny*feather*."

"Pennyfeather sent an extra locker by mistake. He phoned Victor, said he would send a driver to bring the locker back. Fine with Victor. He didn't care.

"Didn't care, that is, until Pennyfeather phoned him back in a panic. 'Is there an ebony raven in the locker?' the prof asked. 'It's priceless, one of a kind. Sheds a whole new light on Edgar Allan Poe. And now I can't find it. I must have put it in the locker by mistake.'

"Victor thought fast. He's sick. He's broke. With extra money he could retire, live out what's left of his life in comfort. 'Haven't seen any raven,' he told Pennyfeather. Then he went back and searched the locker. He found the raven. He got in touch with me. We planned it out. The other day at lunch I followed you to the park. When you stood staring up at the Pendulum, I phoned Victor. He came out and challenged you to make the climb. You know the rest."

"Yeah. You played me."

Hogg smiled wider. He was so sure of himself. He'd known all along he would get the better of me. "Now I'll take the raven and hide it somewhere else.

If you report this to the cops, we will say that *you* stole the raven. That I came up here to do the right thing, to get it back. But it was gone."

He opened the box. He lifted out the cloth bag with the duct tape wound so messily around it.

"Or," he continued, "you can keep the money Victor gave you. Keep quiet. Keep your job at Cliff Edge. Victor and I sell the raven. When that happens, I might even give you a bonus."

He was so *very* sure of himself.

I smiled back at him. I didn't say anything.

He waited. Still I didn't speak. I let the silence grow.

Uneasiness flickered in his eyes. He looked hard at me. He looked down at the package in his hands.

All at once he was tearing at the bubble wrap and the duct tape. He got the top of the bag free. Too impatient to untie the string, he stretched it till it snapped.

He shoved a hand inside the bag and wrenched out—

The skeleton hand of Lenore.

Chapter Fourteen

Hogg glared at me through narrowed eyes. Suddenly he looked a lot like his brother.

He crushed Lenore's hand into tiny pieces. Opening his palm wide, he sprinkled the pieces over the edge of the bar.

Pulling a set of keys from a pocket,

he stuck them one by one between his fingers. He made a fist.

He stepped closer. He stuck out his now-weaponized fist. "Tell me where the raven is."

As if on cue, the raven flew into my mind, twinkly eyed, ebony coat glinting.

And my mind flew too. Back to the previous afternoon.

I was holding the raven in the Pendulum storage room. Varken was shuffling toward me. Snarling at me to put the bird back in the locker.

I couldn't do it. No, it wasn't a real bird.

But whether it was real or not, this bird was different. It had a sense of humor.

Leaning into the locker, I'd grasped Lenore's broken-off hand. I'd dropped it inside the open bag.

With my other hand I'd stuffed the raven into my windbreaker pocket.

I didn't think Varken would guess what I'd done. To be on the safe side, I'd decided to distract him.

Still leaning into the locker, I'd let out a series of blood-curdling yells. Startled, Varken and Pree had jumped back.

I'd told them the yelling came from Lenore. It sounded stupid and crazy. It *was* stupid and crazy.

But my nervousness was genuine. They saw that and they believed me. Pree said something about a lot of the props being mechanized.

From the top of a locker I'd grabbed some duct tape. I'd pretended it was to wrap up the raven securely. What I'd really been doing was making the cloth bag hard to open. Varken thought the raven was inside. I counted on him leaving it safely bound up like that.

I didn't like fooling Pree. When all this was over, I would tell her the truth.

Hogg's words cut through my thoughts, sharp as the keys he brandished.

"Tick, tock, Marlowe. I'm waiting. Tell me where the raven is."

My sock drawer, actually. Rolled up in my windbreaker.

But I wasn't going to tell him that.

I shrugged.

Hogg's bright blue eyes bored into me. Up close, I noticed something about them. They were glacial.

At Cliff Edge, Hogg made like his grumpiness was a joke, an act. But it wasn't. It was the real Hogg.

He clamped a hand on my shoulder, holding me in place. He raised his key-clutching fist.

"*Where is the raven?*"

Wrenching myself free, I shouted, "I'd rather jump than tell you!"

And I did.

Okay, that's not as noble—or stupid—as it sounds.

I didn't jump a hundred feet to the ground.

More like six feet into the Pendulum car. I landed sprawled between two rows of seats.

The *whish*ing sounds from earlier, the ones I hadn't wanted Hogg to notice, had come from the car. From the control booth, Bull had slowly raised it.

The controls had different speed settings. Slow was for maintenance. On that setting the car rose without swinging. It didn't make the ominous *tick, tock.* Just that faint *whish*ing.

Hogg gazed down, stunned. Then he scowled. Six feet wasn't going to stop him. He stepped to the edge of the bar. He was about to jump in after me.

"Bring it down!" I exclaimed.

The car began to descend.

Hogg froze. I saw the abrupt understanding in his eyes, the dismay. I had just spoken to someone–and it wasn't him. Someone else was listening.

Someone had heard Hogg admit to plotting with his brother to steal and sell the raven.

Hogg glanced wildly around, trying to spot the listening device.

I could have told him. Along with a camera, it was wedged under the black metal arch that curved over the horizontal bar.

There was also a camera on the back of the Pendulum car.

I kept quiet. Why spoil someone's fun when they're playing their version of *Where's Waldo?* Besides, the more Hogg looked, the lower the car sank away from him.

The monitoring was a safety thing. As Bull explained it to me, the more you could see and hear, the more you could control.

When I'd told Bull my plan to use my phone's recording app, Bull broke into his loud, howling laughter again. *Why use a phone when we have state-of-the-art equipment?*

Hogg gave up searching. He ran to the footholds. Still fisting the keys, he started climbing down.

He might reach the ground before me.

"Hey, Bull. Speed it up a bit. And call the police."

The car reached the platform. I climbed out.

At the doorway people were straining against the chain. They were bored and angry with waiting. They yelled complaints and obscenities at me.

From the control booth Bull gave

me a thumbs-up. He had phoned the police.

I gave him a return thumbs-up. I glanced at Hogg, still descending the vertical bar. I waved at him. I wanted him to see me. My plan was to run out of there and lead him to the park's entrance.

Security guards hung around the entrance. And the cops should be arriving soon.

But then my plan backfired.

The people waiting behind the chain saw my thumbs-up. They thought I was signaling that the ride was now open.

They broke through the chain and surged up the stairs to the platform.

Way to get trampled. I turned to go down the stairs at the opposite end.

Too late.

From the footholds Hogg pointed

at me. He shouted, "That kid leaving the platform—he's a thief! Stop him!"

People looked from Hogg to me, bewildered. They shifted around and muttered but didn't do anything.

Hogg added the topper.

"*There's a big reward for the person who catches him.*"

That did it. Men, women, teenagers, even little kids charged at me.

Chapter Fifteen

Fists clenched, head lowered in tackle mode, Bull burst out of the control booth. "*Leave Marlowe alone!*"

Nothing scarier than a charging Bull. The crowd halted.

With one exception. Hogg. Nobody was going to get in the way of his and Varken's plans. Especially not the stupid-confident kid he felt superior to.

Hogg shot out his free hand to grab me by the collar. He brandished his key-weaponized fist at Bull. "Erase that recording or I shred your buddy's face."

Bull skidded to a stop. He turned pale. "I—you can't—"

Hogg jammed the tips of the keys into my forehead. Not deep enough to draw blood, but I was pretty sure several arteries were panicking.

People screamed. Would Hogg carry out his threat? I didn't think so. But I wasn't totally sure.

"Okay, okay!" Terrified, Bull lumbered back into the control booth.

What to do? Without that recording there was no evidence. Just my word against Hogg's.

Time was tick-tocking out. If only I could think of something.

I shut my eyes. *I can do this. I can get a grip.*

I took a deep breath. I imagined myself in a climbing situation. I was on a sheer face of rock and I had run out of holds.

Wrong. There had to be a hold somewhere. A bump in the rock, a branch sticking out. The thing was to stay calm, be patient. Like they say, patience gets rewarded.

Rewarded.

That was it. The crowd wanted a reward.

And I had one for them.

I opened my eyes. I pulled the bills out of my pocket, the six hundred I hadn't had the chance to return to Victor. I held them up.

I let the bills flutter to the ground, like butterflies.

The crowd rushed us. In diving for the bills they knocked both Hogg and me over.

I scrambled up first. I stepped down hard on Hogg's wrist. His fingers loosened. He dropped the keys.

I hurled them high over the Pendulum's fence.

Then I ran.

I zoomed through the displays to the Pendulum's entrance. The cops were already there, talking to a frantic Pree.

She had her back to me. She was pointing at a video monitor showing the crowd on the platform.

Near tears, she was jabbering.

"The guy I like is in danger! He's so *brave*, taking on the crowd like that! But now I can't see him, and I'm scared!"

A glow filled me. I straightened my shoulders.

I had a swagger in my step as I walked up to her. Now she was looking at a video screen showing the hallway behind her.

She spun around. She sped toward me. "You're okay! If anything happened to you, I'd..."

She couldn't finish. She choked up.

Nothing that a bear hug couldn't solve. I stretched out my arms.

Except that Pree zoomed past me.

Straight into the arms of—

Bull Bakker.

I pedaled to the university. I locked my bike to the rack with loud, angry clanks. Prisha and Bull. I mean, *Bull*.

Okay, so Bull was a big, muscular, blond guy. If you were into that, fine.

He also had the goofy thing going for him. Maybe that brought out Pree's maternal streak.

The cops had flicked their gazes from my miserable face to Pree's and Bull's happy ones. They weren't cops for nothing. They knew. All the time they questioned me they had pitying looks in their eyes. One of them seemed to be holding back a smile.

Not that they weren't nice. And not that it wasn't satisfying to see them bundle Varken and Hogg into cop cars.

One cop, frowning at the brothers, had asked, "So which of you is Varken and which is Hogg?"

Bull, solemn and trying to be helpful, had said, "They both are both."

Then Prisha had gazed even more adoringly at Bull.

Fine.

Now I looked around the campus. It was quiet in the summer. Just me and a statue of King George VI.

Trees stirred in the breeze. I checked my phone. According to Google Maps, Professor Pennyfeather's office was in a building across from this statue.

I headed over. Too wired to take the elevator, I ran up the stairs.

The professor's door was open. He saw me and smiled.

"Sorry I was so rude the last time I saw you," I said. "I thought you were someone else."

"Not at all! I am glad to see you."

And he rolled his wheelchair around his desk to shake my hand.

Professor Pennyfeather started our conversation off with several sneezes. "Sorry. Clogged sinuses."

He reached into his inside jacket pocket, just like he'd done outside Cliff Edge. At the time, I had been sure he was reaching for a gun.

Now the professor pulled out—an inhaler. He sucked deep breaths from it.

Then he said, "When our truck driver went to the Pendulum to collect the Raven locker, I rode along. Victor Varken wasn't there, but his assistant, Prisha Collins, met us. Very pleasant young woman," he added.

"She has Bull in her life," I said shortly.

"I beg your pardon?" I just shook my head, so Pennyfeather continued. "In any case, pleasant as she was, Prisha was obviously upset about something. I asked her if I could help. She told me she was worried about you, that Varken was forcing you to make a dangerous climb.

"I offered to talk to you. She said you worked across the street. I went over. I should have explained myself better."

I shook my head. "It's not like I gave you a chance. But I hope I can make it up to you."

From my backpack I brought out my rolled-up windbreaker. I pulled the raven out. Its eyes twinkled up at us.

Pennyfeather took the raven and let out a long sigh of relief. "This little beauty belonged to Edgar Allan Poe. It's very precious to me."

I understood. It was kind of how I felt.

Then the professor opened a desk drawer. He took out a gleaming silver letter opener.

He plunged the sharp tip into the raven's head.

Chapter Sixteen

And I'd thought my day could not possibly get worse.

"You wanted the bird back so you could destroy it?" I jumped up. I'd had it with everyone. I was out of here. I was going to go climb some mountaintop and stay up there.

Professor Pennyfeather chuckled. "Not destroy, Conor. The raven was built as a container to hide things in. Like those fake books people stash their jewelry inside. Let me show you."

Pennyfeather held the raven up to me. He had worked the letter opener along a groove that ran from its head to tail.

He explained, "Normally you press down on the groove and the bird opens. But it's been more than a century since Edgar Allan opened the raven. Over time the edges got jammed shut. That's why I had to force the raven open. See? Our little friend is a bit chipped, but not broken."

I wasn't totally satisfied. Still, I was curious. I sat down again.

Pennyfeather nodded, pleased. "Okay. So you know Edgar Allan was famous for his horror writing. In paintings, in old photos, he scowls out at us. He often added to the effect by being wild-eyed and unruly-haired. Whether he intended it or not, this was great marketing—the miserable, haunted writer who gave people nightmares. This is the Edgar Allan we remember."

"The guy who never had a happy day," I said, remembering the woman at the Pendulum displays.

"Except that he did. There was one thing that cheered Edgar Allan up. Cats! He wrote a very funny essay about cats, the way they chase their tails, think so highly of themselves and so on."

I couldn't believe it. The guy who wrote about pendulum blades slicing people up had a sense of humor? "Just checking, sir. This is Edgar Allan *Poe* we're talking about?"

"The same. One day a photographer snapped him with his cat. For whatever reason, Edgar Allan kept the photo a secret. Maybe because it didn't match his public image. Or maybe because it was a private moment he didn't want to share. People of that era thought it improper to smile in photographs. You were supposed to look grim. Ever seen a photo of Queen Victoria? She looks like she just swallowed a spider.

"Regardless of the reason, Poe hid the photo inside an ebony raven he kept on his desk. A few months ago I bought the raven from a Poe collector. It came in a bag of soft cloth, to protect the ebony.

"Then, busy as I am, I made a mistake. I got the bag mixed up with some props. The raven ended up at the amusement park." Pennyfeather glowed. "But you got it back for me, Conor Marlowe. For which I and the university are forever grateful."

He reached into the desk drawer again. But this time not for sharp objects.

For a check.

He handed it to me. Was I seeing right? The amount written on the front made Varken's payment seem like—well, like birdseed.

"Wow," I breathed.

Okay, so Pree liked Bull and not me. Still, it wasn't such a bad day.

Pennyfeather opened the raven wider. The photo was rolled up inside.

The professor unrolled it.

Edgar Allan Poe, fearsome writer of "The Pendulum" and "The Raven," sat with a cat on his lap. Unaware the photographer was taking his picture at that moment, he wore a grin that practically wrapped around his head.

So this was Edgar Allan Poe's secret! Sometimes he knew how to be happy.

I grinned back at the picture. When someone's that happy, you catch it.

And my day had gone from not bad to just fine, thank you.

I realized that being happy meant different things to different people. For Edgar Allan Poe it was cats. For Pree it was a big, goofy, blond guy. For me it's the sun on my face at the top of the Malamute.

Whatever it takes, I say go for it.

Acknowledgments

Thank you, as always, to Orca Book Publishers.

I would be remiss if I didn't also acknowledge Michael Li, my fellow University of Toronto alum, who introduced me to climbing. Thanks to Michael, I got the idea for this book.

Melanie Jackson is the author of several Orca Currents titles, including *Medusa's Scream*, *The Big Dip* and *Fast Slide*. When not writing thrilling tales, she works as a business writer and editor. She lives in Vancouver, British Columbia. For more information, visit melaniejacksonblog.wordpress.com.